Sparks Fly High

The Legend of Dancing Point

Retold by Mary Quattlebaum
Pictures by Leonid Gore

Melanie Kroupa Books
Farrar, Straus and Giroux / New York

Colonel Lightfoot was born with quicksilver feet. No sooner could he stand than he was prancing, no sooner prancing than kicking his baby booties high. His dancing delighted folks for miles around. Why, even the angels in Heaven clapped.

But as he grew, so did his pride.
"Amazing." He applauded his own mincing steps.

"Grand," he cried as he glided.

"My dancing is simply *divine*," he told each lady he twirled 'round the floor.

Oh, the waggy, braggy tongue of the man!

Much as he loved his own waltzing ways, there was one thing the colonel loved more: his land. His fine Virginia land, stretching serene and green along the James River. Whenever he surveyed his beautiful acres, the colonel broke into a jig. He'd wave to neighbors behind their plows. "Poor clodhopping farmers. Their land is as rough as their dancing."

But the colonel himself owned one rough patch of soil—a sad and soggy point. It couldn't be plowed; it couldn't be sowed. Folks wouldn't go near it. Rumor was the devil lived there. On dark, dark nights, you could see his sparks fly high. Sparks struck by flinty hooves on wet, wet ground. Devil sparks.

And each year, as the devil stamped and tramped and sparked and larked, that marsh got bigger and boggier. Why, before you knew it, the whole of Virginia would be nothing but cattails and mud!

The angels were getting worried.

One evening, Colonel Lightfoot donned his finest coat and stockings. He perched his tricorne hat atop his powdered hair. Oh, his shoes shone, his buckles shone, his teeth shone in a happy smile. He was off to the Fairchilds' ball, fully prepared for praise. He opened the door and stepped outside.

Sst! Sssst! Sssssst!

Sparks singed his coat. Sizzled his stockings. Smoked a hole through his hat.

All the shine went out of the colonel. That devil was taunting him, sure enough. Tossing flames this far. Now, that demon had ruined not only his point of land but his dancing clothes as well.

"Devil!" he roared, shaking his fist. Right then and there, Colonel Lightfoot vowed to take back his land. Yes, and put an end to those high-flying sparks. So off he stomped to that swampy point to call on the devil himself.

And the colonel found the big demon, sure enough. Splishing and sparking in a bubbling puddle, making an unholy mess.

"Get . . . off . . . my . . . land!" Colonel Lightfoot yelled till the cattails quaked.

"My dear sir"—the devil smirked—"to what do I owe the honor?"

"My land," said the colonel.

The devil stroked his pointy beard. His gaze slowly swept the man, from sooty shoes to smoky hat. A sly smile slid across his lips. "I'll dance you for it," he said.

Colonel Lightfoot frowned. "This place already belongs to me."

"True," the devil purred, "but you can't plow, sow, or reap a swampy marsh. If you win, I'll turn this patch into a dry and fertile field. And I'll never again harm what is yours. Not one blade of grass. Not one tiny stone."

"And if I lose?"

"Ah," the devil sniggered. "Then *all* your land will be mine forever— murky and muddy and mean."

Colonel Lightfoot threw back his coat and tossed down his hat. "I'll chase you off Virginia soil," he growled, "and down to the fires below."

"Then, my dear sir"—the devil swept him a bow—"may I have this dance?"

The two circled one another. The devil kicked up his heels. The colonel squished a small skip. Soon they were whirling and twirling, jigging and stomping around and around that point.

The devil's eyes gleamed like two hot coals. He'd entered many a contest—and won every one.

Two hours passed.

"Tired?" asked the devil, clicking his hooves.

"Of course not," the colonel snapped. "I'm just used to dancing to music."

"A splendid idea!" The devil clapped his hands.

Bang, bang, bangety-bang. Demons sprang up with their drums. They beat and shrieked and clanged. They raised such a ruckus they scared off the stars. *Bangety-bang-bang-bang.*

The devil laughed and leaped.

But the rhythm confused the colonel. He stumbled and bumbled. He almost fell.

Then *plink* he heard. *Plink. Plink.*

The sound was a soothing rain to his burning ears.

Angels floated above, playing their music. *Plink. Plink. Plink.* It guided his aching toes.

Colonel Lightfoot mopped his brow—and danced on.

Three hours passed. Four.

"Aren't you two finished?" whined a demon.

An angel complained, "I've strummed till my fingers are numb."

Finally, the demons tossed down their sticks and kicked their drums. *Bang*. "We're going home," they snarled.

The angels hitched up their gowns. "Enough is enough," they agreed, wafting away to the clouds.

An eerie silence filled the dark, dark night. The only light came from the devil's sparks, those tiny, high-flying flames.

Colonel Lightfoot was footsore and failing fast. His shoes felt heavy as two—no, *twenty*-two—bricks.

The land was sucking him down. His sweet fields were turning to demon muck.

"My dear sir," the devil purred, "won't you rest for a moment?"

"I'll rest when you do," gasped the colonel.

"Me? Rest?" The devil giggled till fire gushed out his mouth. "I never rest. I am the best at whatever I do. I am amazing. Grand. My dancing's *divine*! No one—least of all a clodhopping farmer—can hope to dance better than me!"

Colonel Lightfoot heard the echo of his own braggy words—and sorrow filled his heart.

Then a thought flashed like a glorious light. Here was the devil's weakness: that flame-spitting dancer was too full of pride.

Colonel Lightfoot heaved a heavy sigh. "I have to admit—you are one fine dancer."

"Fine—ha!" cried the devil, jigging away. "Admit that I am the best."

The colonel stumbled, but managed to stay on his feet. "Your last leap," he said, "was astounding. Would you show it to me again?"

The devil leaped. Up, up, up, with a flick of his hooves. Oh, he was graceful as a goat.

Colonel Lightfoot shook his head. "Seems your other leap was higher."

The devil leaped again.

"Hmmm." The colonel slowed to a shuffle. "High—but not as far."

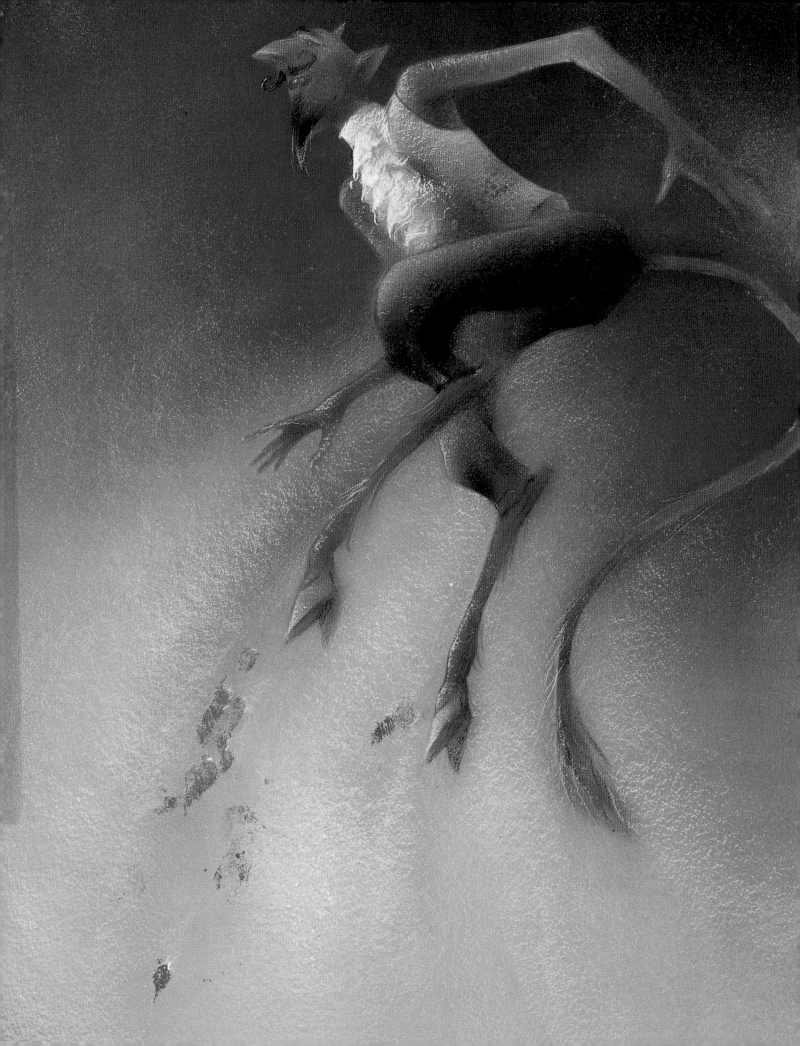

Well, that old devil gritted his teeth. He leaped higher and farther, farther and higher. That night, the folks in Williamsburg swore they saw a shooting star.

"I . . . am . . . the BEST," panted the devil, "at whatever—"

"Your spin," interrupted the colonel, "is not quite as grand as your leap."

"What!" screamed the devil. And he began to spin. Faster, faster, faster.

His spinning sucked the leaves off the trees, the grass from the ground. Even the horses in far-off Fredericksburg got flung mane over tail.

That blazing wind caught Colonel Lightfoot and tossed him like a twig. Still, the man managed to shout, "That's a mighty spin, devil, indeed it is. But your skip seems a little . . . slow."

"*Slow!*" shrieked the devil. "I'll show you—"

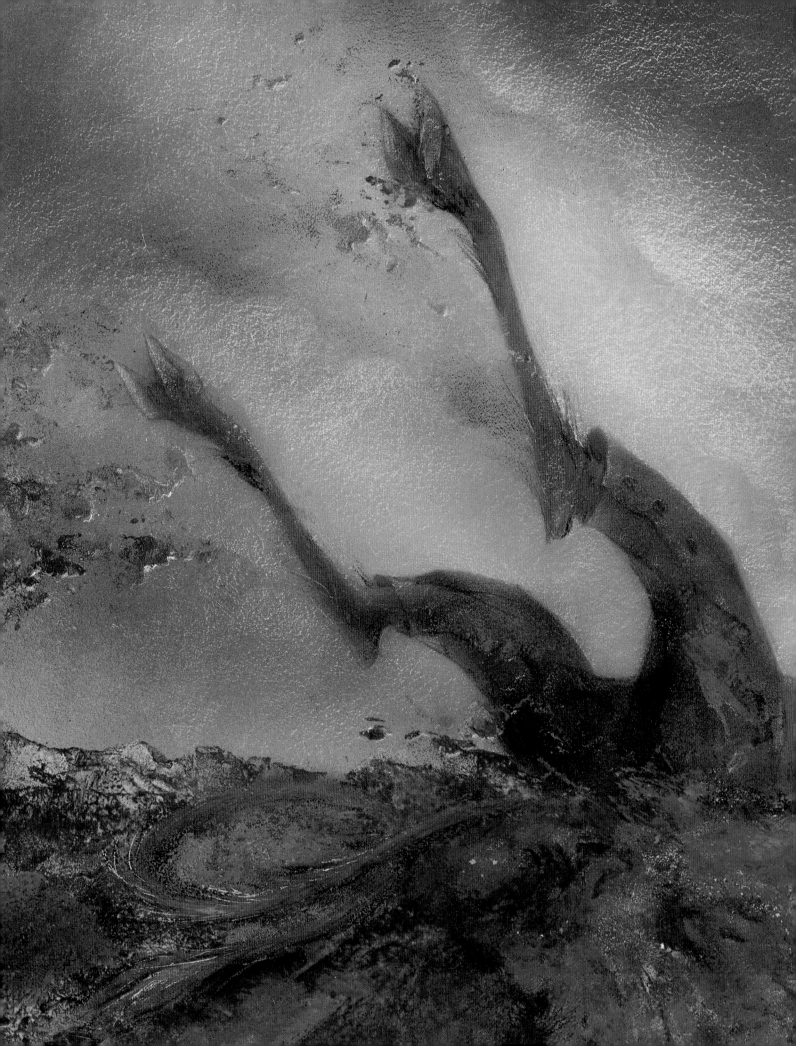

But his words were lost forever. At that moment, the devil fell flat in a
wheezing faint, with his hooves stuck straight in the air.

The colonel knuckled his tired eyes . . . then crumpled to the ground.

When Colonel Lightfoot awoke, he was lying in a dry and fertile field with the noon sun beaming above. His shoes were nothing but two muddy buckles. An ash heap smoldered nearby.

That's when he knew: the devil had turned the marshy point into plowable land—and slunk down to the fires below.

Colonel Lightfoot creaked to his knees to say a thankful prayer. He saluted the harp-playing angels. Then he limped home and slept for three days straight.

And at the next dance he was a new man. Modest as a sparrow. The colonel could still mince the daintiest minuets. He could still romp through the most rollicking reel. But he was quick to praise the steps of others and never applauded his own.

All that happened a long time ago, but the Virginia point never completely recovered. While most is fertile ground, smack in the middle is a big, barren circle. Colonel Lightfoot and the devil had stomped all the life out of that one place. Folks now call it "Dancing Point."

But on dark, dark nights, you might see . . . well, *sparks* flying there. The kind the devil can strike.

And if you look close, you might make out two shadows. Two shadows leaping. Spinning. Kicking their heels.

If you see such a sight, you'll know what it is—a dance contest.

See, the devil could never admit he had lost.

And the colonel's ghost is happy to keep him busy. Happy to keep him from making another unholy mess.

"Hmmm," you might hear Colonel Lightfoot murmur, "your last leap, I believe, was a little bit higher."

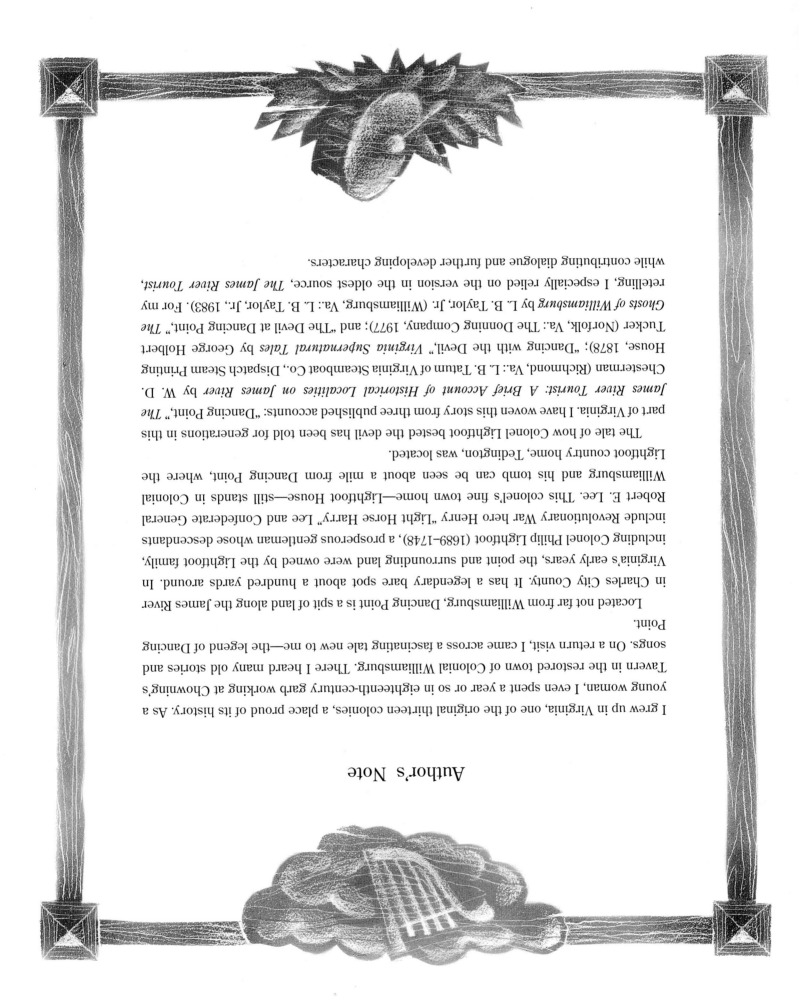

Author's Note

I grew up in Virginia, one of the original thirteen colonies, a place proud of its history. As a young woman, I even spent a year or so in eighteenth-century garb working at Chowning's Tavern in the restored town of Colonial Williamsburg. There I heard many old stories and songs. On a return visit, I came across a fascinating tale new to me—the legend of Dancing Point.

Located not far from Williamsburg, Dancing Point is a spit of land along the James River in Charles City County. It has a legendary bare spot about a hundred yards around. In Virginia's early years, the point and surrounding land were owned by the Lightfoot family, including Colonel Philip Lightfoot (1689–1748), a prosperous gentleman whose descendants include Revolutionary War hero Henry "Light Horse Harry" Lee and Confederate General Robert E. Lee. This colonel's fine town home—Lightfoot House—still stands in Colonial Williamsburg and his tomb can be seen about a mile from Dancing Point, where the Lightfoot country home, Tedington, was located.

The tale of how Colonel Lightfoot bested the devil has been told for generations in this part of Virginia. I have woven this story from three published accounts: "Dancing Point," *The James River Tourist: A Brief Account of Historical Localities on James River* by W. D. Chesterman (Richmond, Va.: L. B. Tatum of Virginia Steamboat Co., Dispatch Steam Printing House, 1878); "Dancing with the Devil," *Virginia Supernatural Tales* by George Holbert Tucker (Norfolk, Va.: The Donning Company, 1977); and "The Devil at Dancing Point," *The Ghosts of Williamsburg* by L. B. Taylor, Jr. (Williamsburg, Va.: L. B. Taylor, Jr., 1983). For my retelling, I especially relied on the version in the oldest source, *The James River Tourist*, while contributing dialogue and further developing characters.

In memory of Lisa and those fun days in Williamsburg
—M.Q.

With thanks to Melanie Kroupa
for helping my creative sparks fly high
—L.G.

Acknowledgments

My gratitude goes to Gregory Stoner, of the Virginia Historical Society, for his cheerful help in tracking down sources, and to Christopher and Christy David for their wonderful support and for our adventurous trek to Dancing Point. I'd like to sweep a big thank-you bow to my agent, Jennifer Carlson, and editor, Melanie Kroupa, for helping to dance this story into print. And fondest thanks "for the memories" to the whole crew, especially Joyce Jones, Murray Unruh Edwards, Jenny Shaffer, Carolyn Wolsifer, and Jim and Jean Puckett, at Chowning's Tavern in Colonial Williamsburg, and to Williamsburg buddies Kathy Dobbs Erskine, Dolly Astin Mayerchak, and Lisa Thompson Slover.
—M.Q.

Distributed in Canada by Douglas & McIntyre Ltd.
Color separations by Chroma Graphics PTE Ltd.
Printed and bound in China by South China Printing Co. Ltd.
Designed by Jay Colvin
First edition, 2006
1 3 5 7 9 10 8 6 4 2

www.fsgkidsbooks.com

Library of Congress Cataloging-in-Publication Data
Quattlebaum, Mary.
    Sparks fly high: the legend of Dancing Point / retold by Mary Quattlebaum;
pictures by Leonid Gore.— 1st ed.
        p.   cm.
    Summary: When Colonel Lightfoot and the devil hold a lengthy dance contest to
see who will control a plot of land along the James River in Virginia, the result is a
surprise for both participants.
    ISBN-13: 978-0-374-34452-8
    ISBN-10: 0-374-34452-3
    [1. Dance—Folklore. 2. Devil—Folklore. 3. Contests—Folklore. 4. Folklore—
Virginia.] I. Gore, Leonid, ill. II. Title.
PZ8.1.Q3 Wh 2006
398.2 E 22
                                                                                        2005042921